MW00930057

Other Children's Book Recommendation

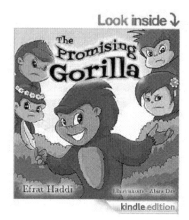

The Sparkling Red Shoes

Miley Smiley

kindle edition

Why do turtles have a Shell?

NEW

By S. Adler

Illustrated by Abira Das

kindle edition

Unique in a Wonderful Way

WRITTEN BY KATE HART
ILLUSTRATED BY JASMINE MILLS

kindle edition

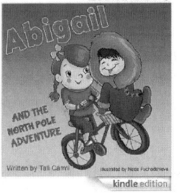

Abigail

AND THE NORTH POLE ADVENTURE

Written by Tali Carmi

Illustrated by Neda Fuchadzhieva

kindle edition

THE CLUEFINDERS CLUB SPECIAL 1

—THE CASE OF THE— DISAPPEARING DE MILO

Introduction

Beatrix, Clara, Christopher and Benjamin, They called themselves the Cluefinders Club.

So for years they had been meeting after school. They called themselves the Cluefinders Club.

The best friends would teach themselves how to be detectives, by finding clues and following the trail until the mystery was solved.

Content

PART ONE: A TUNNEL UNDER THE SEA

It was the first week in October, and the weather was blustery and cold. Even though the wind made everybody shiver, nature had made up for it by making all the leaves on the trees beautiful shades of red, orange and yellow. The sun always seemed to be lower in the sky, filling the air with warm light. As the air got colder, people in the street got friendlier, grateful for every smile.

Clara, Beatrix, Chris and Ben were on a coach, looking out the window as the city rushed by. The four friends were on a school trip. The whole coach was full of kids from their school, and several teachers including Mister Faraday and Miss Marshall. It was very noisy with all those children in the same place, laughing and joking, playing games, teasing one another, and singing along to music from their phones.

They were going on a very special trip. The coach would take them all the way across England to the coast, and from there they would board a train that would go through an underground tunnel. The tunnel would take them into another country altogether – France.

"How will we get onto the train?" asked Chris, who was a big fan of trains. "Is there a train station at the coast?"

"No," said Mister Faraday, smiling. He had recently shaved off his famous moustache, so he still looked strange to the kids. "We're going to drive the coach *onto* the train!"

"What! Really!?"

The kind teacher nodded. "This is a special train, on its very own track. It goes right *under* the English Channel."

"What's that, sir?"

"The English Channel is a patch of the sea that separates the island of Great Britain from the rest of Europe. The French have a different name for it in their own language, of course!"

Clara looked frightened. "So the tunnel goes *under the sea!?*"

"That's right," said Mister Faraday. "But don't worry, it's perfectly safe! And it means we don't have to get a boat to sail across. The train is a special train, called the Eurostar—"

"I know all about the Eurostar!" said Chris. "It's quite famous! It's built so that cars can drive onto it, and it takes them all the way from England to France, and back again!"

Chris was very excited. He really liked to travel on trains, which he thought were super fun – even though the last time they'd been on a train, it had gone out of control and raced halfway across the countryside before they could stop it! That had been one of the Cluefinders Club's earliest mysteries, which they'd solved with great style.

The Cluefinders Club was the name of their little group: Chris, Clara, Ben and Beatrix. They loved to play detective. Sometimes they even had a real mystery to solve! It was often very exciting. There was also a new member of the club: Spooky, Ben's dog. But Spooky had to be left at home. He wasn't allowed to go on a school trip to France!

When the coach got close to the coast, the kids all pressed against the windows to look out.

"I can see the seaside!" said Beatrix happily. "Oh, I wish we could go to the beach! I love wading in the water."

"I like reading on the beach with a cold drink!" said Clara.

"I like building sandcastles," said Chris, and then he and Ben starting arguing about whose sandcastles were the best.

Miss Marshall, the new teacher at Upton School, smiled and handed out juice boxes to all the kids. "Isn't it exciting enough to be going to Paris in France?" she asked. "You can go to the seaside any time!"

"It *is* exciting, Miss!" said Clara. "I heard that Paris is the most romantic city in the world."

The two teachers, Mister Faraday and Miss Marshall, shared a secret look between them. Mister Faraday smiled and said, "I should think you're too young to be thinking about romance, Clara! But you like looking at paintings, right? There are some amazing galleries in Paris. It was one of the artistic capitals of the world."

"I can't wait!" said Clara.

"I want to eat lots of pizza and pasta!" said Ben, rubbing his tummy.

Chris poked him in the shoulder. "That's Italy, stupid! French specialities are tasty bread and pastries, and lots of different types of cheeses! I hope we get there soon, I'm starting to feel hungry!"

Soon enough, their coach got to the front of a long line of cars and buses. They entered the Channel Tunnel and drove right onto a special platform attached to a long train. Once it was fully loaded with lots of passengers, cars and buses, the train set off on its journey under the water.

Clara was a little scared by the idea at first. She thought the tunnel might crack and millions of tonnes of water would crash down onto them. But Ben reminded her that some very clever people had specially designed and built the tunnel; they used mathematics to calculate exactly how strong it would need to be, making it perfectly safe. Clara was a little more relaxed after this, and even though the tunnel was dark, the coach had its inside lights switched on. They carried on chatting and joking as usual, the members of the Cluefinders Club debating which of the recent Sherlock Holmes films they liked the best.

The teachers had all the pupils quieten down, and then told them some interesting things about France. The children learned that more people went on holiday to France than any other country in the world. Even though France was a really big country, three quarters of the people living there were in cities, not spread out over the beautiful countryside. And some of the world's cleverest philosophers came from there, but none of the children could pronounce their names: Descartes, Pascal, Voltaire, Baudelaire, Sartre...

"Why can't they have simple names, like Smith?" joked Ben, but really he was impressed by everything he heard about France. It sounded like a wonderful, interesting country.

And after just half an hour on the train, they were there!

PART TWO: THE VENUS DE MILO

They were out of the tunnel and back into the open air. The scenery didn't look much different, but somehow the children could *feel* that they were in a new place. A new country!

"We're near a city called Calais in France," said Mister Faraday. It was pronounced "Kal-ay". He told them that they would be on the coach for another three hours before they reached Paris, which was the capital city of France.

The children groaned, but actually the time passed pretty quickly, and soon they were in the wonderful city of Paris.

They looked out of the windows at the beautiful city. The buildings were very elegant with many windows and balconies, some of which had flowers and birdcages on them. They passed some big hotels, which looked very grand with flagpoles and expensive cars nearby. There were a lot of restaurants and cafés, where people sat outside for hours sipping coffee and chatting. Many streets had trees lining them, and at one point they caught a glimpse of the Eiffel Tower, the famous tall monument of Paris that they had seen in so many films.

The class would be staying at special lodgings just outside the city. It was a place designed for school classes, and had lots of bunk beds. The boys would be sleeping in separate rooms from the girls, and there was a cafeteria where they would have breakfast in the morning.

Once they'd dropped off all their bags, it was time to explore Paris!

First the class went to the Arc de Triomph (Mister Faraday pronounced it "tree-omff"). It was a special structure at the end of a long road called Champs-Élysées ("shonz ell-eez-ay"). The structure was a large arch made of stone and beautifully carved with lots of tiny pictures and words. It was built to pay respect to French soldiers. Even though the children wondered if it had a practical purpose, they still thought it was very impressive.

After that, they all went to a big café and had lunch. There was a lot to choose from. Most of the kids had *steak en frites*, which was steak and French fries. The teachers had some weird-sounding food: onion soup, mussels, and something called "escargot" that looked suspiciously like snails!

"All right!" said Miss Marshall, clapping her hands after they had all finished eating their food. "We have a special afternoon planned. A friend of mine is one of the curators at the Louvre, and we all have special passes to visit this afternoon and tomorrow to explore."

"Miss," said Darren, one of the other kids. "What's the Loov?"

"It's a museum here in Paris where some of the world's most special and important pieces of art are kept. Has anyone heard of the Mona Lisa, a painting by Leonard da Vinci? Or of the famous statue, the Venus de Milo? These are kept at the Louvre museum, which is well-known all around the world. A curator is a person who looks after a museum. We're really lucky to get some special time at the end of the day and even after it usually closes. I'll pass out some brochures in your groups, and you can decide which areas you want to go to first in the museum."

The four best friends huddled around their brochure.

"Wow, it's ginormous!" said Clara. "They must have a million things here!"

"I want to look at the French paintings!" said Beatrix.

"I want to look at the Ancient Egypt section!" said Chris.

In the end, they settled to look at the paintings first and the old things from Egypt that had been dug out of the ground later. Chris loved that people all around the world were digging for ancient artefacts that could show us what life was like two thousand years ago!

They spent many hours exploring the museum. There was always a teacher or a tour guide with them to keep them safe, but the children hardly noticed the grown-ups that lingered nearby.

Near the end of the day, people were being asked to make their way to the exits. The museum was closing for the day. Luckily the school had special passes, and they were all brought together to see some of the most special and interesting things as a class.

Mister Faraday and Miss Marshall led them into a long room lined with very old, beautiful paintings. In the middle, on a special wall, was a smallish painting of a dark-haired woman.

"Has anyone seen a picture of this painting before?" asked Mister Gervais, the museum curator. He was the person who looked after the whole museum and made sure it ran well, keeping people happy and looking after the exhibits. He was a friend of Miss Marshall's.

Clara put up her hand. "Sir, that's called the Mona Lisa," she said.

"Very good!" said Mister Gervais. "It was painted by an important Italian artist and architect named Leonardo da Vinci."

"She looks a bit sad," said Ben. "I wonder why?"

Later they were shown a wide room that was bright with sunlight coming through large glass windows. There were paintings and statues, and at the far end was another important piece of art. It was a white marble statue of a woman named the Venus de Milo.

"She's got no arms!" laughed Chris. "Why did they make a statue with no arms?"

"This beautiful sculpture wasn't intended to look this way," said Mister Gervais, looking lovingly at the armless woman. "The statue was broken a long time ago. She was found this way on the island of Milos in Greece, which is where she gets the second part of her name. The first part of her name, Venus, was a Roman name for the goddess of love. And doesn't she look lovely?"

Ben crossed his arms. "I don't see what's so special about it. Just because it's old? If I broke a statue nowadays, we'd throw it away and get a new one..."

"I don't think that's the point, Benjamin," whispered Mister Faraday.

Mister Gervais said, "Try to imagine, everybody, how long it took for the artist Alexandros to chip away with a tiny chisel and hammer at a huge piece of marble, working minute by minute with this beautiful goddess in his imagination. After many weeks and months, the lump of stone would turn into this incredible piece of art. He must have been extraordinarily patient and talented."

After Ben thought about it, he agreed. "Actually, that *is* pretty cool!"

"If that's not enough," said the smiling Mister Gervais, "think about this – the Venus de Milo is worth so much money that it's impossible to put a price on it!"

"Wow," said Chris. "That's a lot!"

And he was right, but it was now time to leave. Their extra half an hour in the closed museum had come to an end, so it was time to go to the special lodgings outside the city.

PART THREE: "THERE'S A MYSTERY TO BE SOLVED!"

The lodgings were very fun. Although the four best friends had many sleepovers in the past, they'd never all slept in bunkbeds away from home before.

The boys immediately jumped up onto the top bunks. The girls were happy on the bottom – everybody got their preference! As the boys threw paper aeroplanes at each other from their high-up beds, the girls sat close and talked quietly about all the interesting things they'd seen and practised saying some words in French.

After supper, it was time to go to bed. They turned out the lights and settled under their sheets, heads on comfy pillows. The four friends whispered to each other in the darkness.

"Chris? The Egyptians were really awesome, weren't they?" said Ben with a giant yawn.

"Yeah ... I wish we lived in Ancient Egyptian times."

Beatrix said, "No you don't ... It was probably horrible compared to today. You would probably be a slave!"

Chris chuckled sleepily. "I would miss my iPod."

"There would be no school trips to Paris," murmured Clara. "Paris probably didn't exist back then ... Or Italy. Or the Venus de Milo..."

They soon drifted off to sleep, dreaming about the magnificent history of the world.

In the morning, the class of twenty students had breakfast together with the teachers. They were told that before the Louvre opened at 9 o'clock French time (the clocks were an hour ahead compared to back in England), they would be able to spend another special half an hour with the curator, Mister Gervais.

But when they got there, disaster had struck!

Miss Marshall couldn't find her friend Mister Gervais anywhere.

"He must be busy getting things ready," she said. "All the curators are extremely busy."

Somebody allowed them to look around the museum anyway, as they had special permission from Mister Gervais. They picked up where they left off, exploring paintings and statues and ancient relics of times gone by.

The four friends decided to go back to the Venus de Milo. They just felt that there was something special and different about that statue, even though it was old and broken. Both the boys and the girls thought that 'Venus' was beautiful (Although Clara wished she'd put on some clothes).

But when they got to the wide, exquisitely designed room where the Venus de Milo was, they found Mister Gervais and lots of policeman standing around an empty space.

"I can't believe it!" said Beatrix. "Something's happened to the statue!"

Just then, Miss Marshall walked in behind them with some of the other students. She went to talk to Mister Gervais, who seemed very upset. He was a small man with a round tummy, and his face was usually bright with a wide smile, but today he looked unhappy and small, as though it was the worst day of his life.

Then the teacher came back to talk to the children. "I'm afraid we'll have to gather the other kids and leave. The Venus de Milo has been stolen!"

"No!" exclaimed Ben. "But everything looks so safe and secure here! How could someone steal it overnight?"

Miss Marshall smiled. "Well, luckily it's not up to me to figure it out! It's up to those policemen now. We'd better get out of their way and let them do their job."

"Maybe we can help?" suggested Clara. "The Cluefinders Club has solved plenty of mysteries in its time!"

"Oh, has it really?" said the amused teacher. "Well, this isn't quite the same as a vanishing schoolgirl. Come on, let's go and find everybody else."

The four amateur detectives really wanted to stay, but they had to listen to their teacher. As they were led back the way they'd come, Chris and Ben swapped a secret look ... Beatrix saw them, and gasped. Those cheeky boys were up to something!

Just as Miss Marshall turned the corner, Ben quietly hid behind a statue.

Beatrix moved her lips without speaking out loud. "*What are you doing!?*"

"Shhh!" he whispered. "There's a mystery to be solved!"

Ben was always doing things like this! Why couldn't he just do as he was told?

Ben was by himself. He waited until the others were out of sight, then sneaked out from behind the statue. He could hear the voices of the curator and the policemen speaking in French. If only he could understand what they were saying!

He crept around the corner, then tip-toed from statue to statue, hiding all the time. No-one saw him. He thought he was being very clever! "Maybe I should be a burglar?" he thought. "No, I could never do that! People who steal things are horrible. Better that I be a detective!"

Ben found a nearby statue and crouched behind it. He was close to where the Venus de Milo should have been. There was a tall block, which was called a plinth, that the statue used to stand on. But only the plinth was left, with a bare patch where the statue used to stand.

One of the policeman had some large, shiny photographs. They looked like they'd been taken from a security camera. It showed three men moving the statue. A fourth man in a long black coat and a black hat watched them. He seemed to be the mastermind behind the theft.

Mister Gervais bent down to pick something up from behind the plinth. It was a small piece of paper.

Ben tried to get closer. He tip-toed from behind one statue to another. Then he could see more clearly. Mister Gervais had found a ticket. And there was a little picture on it, a tall triangle shape ... The Eiffel Tower!

The policemen went to move the heavy plinth to see if there were any more clues. As they did so, a cloud of dust rose up into the air. Ben couldn't help it. The dust went up his nose. His eyes started to water.

"Uhhh..." he said, grabbing his nose, but there was nothing he could do. He sneezed, so loudly that it echoed around the whole room. "*AHHH-CHOOOOO!*"

Mister Gervais and the policemen nearly jumped a mile into the air! They whirled around, shocked, to see Ben crouching behind a statue of a lady holding a shield. Ben didn't know what else to do – so he ran as fast as he could!

"Hey, boy!" shouted a policeman in accented English.

Ben heard the kind curator say, "It's okay, it's just one of the school children from this morning."

Phew!

Ben ran around the corner and caught up with Miss Marshall and the others.

"Did you see anything?" asked Clara in a whisper. "What happened?"

"I'll tell you what happened, Cluefinders!" whispered Ben excitedly. "We have a clue!"

PART FOUR: A TRIP TO THE TOWER

The teachers told them that they would be visiting the famous Eiffel Tower that day.

"Perfect!" Ben whispered to his friends. "That's where the clue leads us. The thief dropped a ticket to the Eiffel Tower."

Clara tutted. "Ben, you're not using your brain. If he had a ticket, then *he's already been* there! We won't find him."

"That's where you're wrong! The ticket hadn't been torn or hole-punched, like any other ticket. I think he was *planning* to go – maybe today!"

Beatrix clapped her hands. "Perfect! Well done, Ben! When we go, we will have to keep an eye out for a man in a black coat and hat."

But it wasn't going to be that easy!

When the coach pulled out to the wide open space that featured the Tower, they saw how big it really was. Chris had already gathered some facts about it from Miss Marshall, who used to live in Paris.

"It's as high as a building with eighty floors!" he said. "It's the tallest structure in the whole city. It's the tallest man-made thing in the whole world, higher than the skyscrapers in America!"

The Tower was wide at the bottom and pointed at the top, a bit like a space rocket. The bottom had four legs that turned into arches where they joined. Then the tower got narrower and narrower as it rose up above the treetops, above the buildings ... it looks like it could poke the clouds with its sharp tip! It was made of lots of criss-crossing metal bars that made it really strong and sturdy.

"It's *massive!*" exclaimed Beatrix. "Can we go up it?"

Mister Faraday was handing out the tickets he'd just bought at the booth. The queue had been very, very long. Everyone else had gotten an ice cream to pass the time on the great lawn that stretched out from the feet of the tower.

He said, "You *can* go up it, Beatrix! There's a lift that goes up the middle, right to the top, or there are lots and *lots* of stairs. Guess how many?"

"A hundred!" said Chris immediately.

"Nope," said Mister Faraday. "Try again!"

"Two hundred?" guessed Clara.

"No – six hundred! And that's only to the second level out of three!"

Chris scratched his head. "Um, I think we should get the lift instead! Thanks for the offer though!"

All the school children got into one giant lift. They went up and up. It seemed to take forever! But with every second they got higher and higher over the city, until they could see far over the trees and Metro lines, and see all the buildings of the city lit in the bright sunlight, and the city's many green areas.

"I'm not sure I want to go any higher..." said Clara. "I'm a bit scared of heights."

"It's totally safe," Ben whispered. "I'll make sure you're okay. Promise!"

Clara felt better after that, and even held Ben's hand for a while.

At the second level there was a whole restaurant, and even a small museum. They looked at pictures of how the Eiffel Tower had been built. It was an amazing achievement.

Just then, Beatrix thought she saw something amongst the crowds. Of all the hundreds of people on the Tower at that moment, she'd seen a man in a black coat sat at the restaurant sipping a coffee and reading a newspaper with great interest. He had a black hat on the table next to him.

"Guys!" Beatrix whispered, getting the other Cluefinders' attention. "I think it's the thief!"

They huddled around a corner and watched the man read his newspaper. He was flicking through the pages very fast, as though looking for something specific amongst the papers. When he couldn't find it he looked angry, and slapped the folded newspaper onto the table.

"He looks mad," Chris commented. "Maybe he thought his burglary was going to be in the newspaper?"

Clara said, "It should be, shouldn't it? The Venus de Milo is famous all around the world. Why wouldn't the newspapers mention it?"

"Maybe they haven't had time to put it in this morning's newspaper," said Ben, who always read the paper after his Dad had finished with it. "Or maybe the Louvre is keeping it a secret for now?"

"Look, he's finished his coffee!"

The man stood up and put on his black hat. He was tall and quite thin, and his angry face made him look quite menacing. He wore large glasses. He left the crumpled newspaper on the table and walked away quickly.

"Should we follow him?" asked Beatrix.

"What would we do if we caught up to him? We need evidence," said Chris.

They ran up to the table the man had been sitting at. He'd left some bits of rubbish there he didn't think he needed anymore. There was the newspaper, a paper napkin stuffed into his coffee cup, his ticket for the Eiffel Tower – this one with a hole punched in it – and a folded bit of cardboard.

"What's this?" said Ben, picking it up. It was only about an inch long and had glossy images on the front.

"It's a matchbook," said Chris. "My Mum used to have some when she used to smoke. The little book has matches inside, and you break them off when you need them. When all the matches are gone, you throw the wrapper away. I'm glad she stopped smoking – it was disgusting!"

Ben was looking at the matchbook. It had the name of a hotel written on it: L'HOTEL NOTRE DAME.

"What does this mean?" he asked. "Isn't Notre Dame that famous church?"

"It's a cathedral," Clara corrected. "It's been around for a very long time. This hotel must have been named after the cathedral – so it must be near to it. Do you think that's where the man in black is staying?"

"It could be," said Beatrix seriously. "I wish we could go there and find out."

Just then, a man said loudly, "You there!"

The children looked up. It was a policeman! He had dark hair and a big moustache, much bigger than Mister Faraday's. He wore a long beige-coloured coat and had some regular policeman behind him. The children knew enough about mystery stories to know that he was a detective.

"I'm Detective Flambergé," he said, pronouncing it 'flam-ber-zhey'. "You were the children at the museum this morning, correct?"

He looked directly at Ben, who said nothing. He thought that he was in trouble! The Detective saw the matchbook in Ben's hand and quickly took it. "So, you thought you'd followed the thief here, did you? Leave the detective work to the professionals, little boy. We know what we're doing."

And with that, he turned around and told everybody to move away from the coffee table. They must have seen the man in black sitting there from a distance, and knew there might be more clues around. The children had no choice but to leave.

"We're never going to get anywhere with this," said Beatrix sadly. "We don't know the city, and we don't speak French. We can't even go by ourselves to follow the clues, because the teachers won't let us."

That was when Miss Marshall gathered all the children back into the elevator to tell them where they were going next.

She said, "Who's heard of the Notre Dame cathedral?"

PART FIVE: THE UNHAPPY HUNCHBACK

So the next part of their school trip would take them to Notre Dame! The four Cluefinders thought this was very lucky, but how would they be able to sneak away to investigate the hotel and find the thief?

Their coach carried the class along the bank of the river Seine, which ran through Paris. This part of the city was beautiful; many arching bridges stretched over the wide, slow-moving river, and the promenade was lined with many tiny stalls selling books, books and more books. Clara instantly wanted to stop the coach and go shopping.

Mister Faraday chuckled. "There's a good reason why it might not be worth your time looking for books here, Clara. Why do you think that is?"

She thought about it for a while. She loved reading, and she loved books, and she had some pocket money in her purse, so why wouldn't it be worth her time? Then she realised: she was in France...

"...So all the books will be written in French!" she said.

"That's right," said Mister Faraday. "Well done!"

Clara couldn't read French, but as she saw those hundreds and hundreds of books laid out in the sunshine, she really wished she could! Imagine all the many stories in those old pages, a thousand mysteries to be solved and a million characters to meet and come to love.

"Don't worry," said Ben, seeing her sad face. "We'll be back home tomorrow, and you have a hundred books waiting for you in your bedroom!"

Clara smiled. It was true! And besides, who wanted to read when there was a real mystery to be solved?

The Notre Dame cathedral sat on a small island in the middle of the river. The river widened and then split, leaving a little bit of land in the middle, and then joined back up again at the back. There was enough room on the island for the grand church-like building, a few hotels and shops, and of course, plenty of cafés. "If there's one thing that the French love, it's to sip coffee and watch the world go by," said Miss Marshall.

When the children saw Notre Dame, they thought their heads would fall off! It was no bigger than a regular church back in England, but it was absolutely beautiful, with two big towers on either side, a giant door at the front, and a huge round window made of stained class in a hundred different colours. There was a large spire in the middle and lots of little towers and archways, called buttresses, and of course many smaller windows. The overall effect was of something very old and magnificent, a spiky building that seemed to suck in light from all directions and glow magically.

"The people who built it must have really been in love with it," said Beatrix, in awe. "You can tell that they wanted to make it perfect. And I think it is!"

Miss Marshall told them some interesting things about it. "Notre Dame means 'Our Lady', named after Mary from the Bible story. Inside there is a giant organ, which is a bit like a piano but with giant metal tubes sticking out the top. It makes really deep, powerful music that choirs like to sing holy songs to. And do you know about the famous bells? Inside the towers are five enormous bells that ring out the time and on special occasions. One of them weighs thirteen tons, which is about the same as seven cars!"

As the class piled out of the coach, eager to see more of the fascinating building, the four friends wondered how they might slip away. But there was no opportunity, because the teachers were very good at taking care of their class. It would be very bad if they lost a child!

And so Ben, Beatrix, Clara and Chris followed the teachers through the huge doors and into the glorious space of the inner cathedral.

"I feel funny," said Beatrix, touching her chest. "There's a special air in here."

She whispered, because it was so quiet. Every little noise seemed like a big one. They felt it would be disrespectful to be loud, for some reason. Everyone felt it.

"Maybe because it's a place where only good people come, the old stones have filled with positive feelings?" suggested Chris. "I know it sounds strange, but I bet that's it. It feels like it's not *just* a building, but nobody lives here except a bunch of statues!"

The class explored the inside of the cathedral. But Ben was anxious to follow the matchbook clue and find the thief.

They crept into a little corner to talk about it. There was a stairwell, which was a narrow spiral of stairs that went up into one of the towers. The door was shut, but they sneaked inside to talk in private.

"What should we do?" asked Ben, sitting on one of the stairs in the low light. "I'm sure that Detective will find the missing Venus de Milo, but what if he can't? What if we're the only ones who find the one clue that solve the case? We have to try!"

They heard a noise coming from up the staircase. The stairs were a twisting spiral, so there was no way to see up to the top. They could only wonder.

Then the noise came again. It sounded like someone going *pssst!*

"Is that a person?" asked Clara. "But I thought the cathedral was usually empty, except for visitors downstairs? I didn't think people were allowed to go up the towers."

"Well, there's definitely *something* up there!" said Chris.

"What if it's a ghost?" asked Clara. "A lot of these old buildings are supposed to be haunted..."

"I doubt it," said Ben. "Remember what happened when we thought my house was haunted, and it turned out to just be Spooky?"

They all smiled to remember the first time they'd met the little puppy. It had been a frightening mystery, but in the end there had been nothing to worry about.

"Let's go and see," Beatrix suggested with a bright smile. "If there's nothing there, at least we might be able to see that hotel from the top of the tower!"

"If that's *your* idea, then I think you should go *first!*" said Clara, giving her friend a playful nudge.

Beatrix put her hand against the curved wall and started the slow climb up the spiralling stairs of Notre Dame's tower...

They climbed and climbed the stairs. They went on for so long that their legs went tired and wobbly. By the time they got to the top, Chris fell onto his back and lay there for a while, groaning.

Ben, who was quite sporty, was jogging on the spot with a big cheesy grin on his face. "What? That wasn't a lot of stairs! You three need to get more exercise!"

Before he could say another word, a low voice from somewhere in the tower said, "Three hundred and eighty seven."

The four kids nearly jumped out of their skins! There was a person in the tower with them!

"Wh-who's there?" asked Clara nervously. "Come out!"

They were in a small room with stone floor and walls, and a wide space in the floor that went right down the centre of the tower. They were in a bell tower, and above the wide space hung a giant bell, the one that Miss Marshall had mentioned. It was enormous and clearly very old.

The voice had come from behind a giant bell. As they watched, a shy young man crept out into the sunlight through the narrow window. He had shaggy brown hair and a lumpy but honest face. His back was very crooked, and he had a big hump on his shoulder beneath his clothes. At first the children thought he was ugly, but the moment he stepped forward they saw he was very friendly.

His giant smile put them at ease. "Sorry to scare you! I know that I'm hideous to look at, but I don't mean you any harm."

Clara was still a little afraid, but Beatrix was quick to put out her hand for him to shake. "You're too harsh on yourself! We're sorry to barge in here without knocking, but we thought we heard you give a *pssst*!"

"I did, and thank you all for coming up! My name is Quasimodo, and I've lived in this tower for a long time. I was abandoned as a baby and brought here, where my ugliness wouldn't upset the people of the city."

"That's so sad!" said Chris. "But there are lots of ugly people, you won't stand out that much."

Beatrix elbowed him hard in the ribs. She whispered, "You don't have to *agree* that he's ugly! Be polite, we're in his home after all."

"It's okay," said Quasimodo. "Really, I just love to be here with the bells and the gargoyles. They're my friends. And I adore Paris and everything in it. That's why I was shocked to hear you say that the Venus de Milo had been stolen from the Louvre! Is this true!?"

"I'm afraid it is," said Ben. "We've been trying to find the thief, a man who wears a black coat and hat, but we haven't had much luck. The only clue we have is a matchbook that suggests he might be staying at a place called L'Hotel Notre Dame."

Quasimodo smiled and nodded. "Your pronunciation is quite good! You would fit right in here in Paris. And I think I know that hotel – come with me, please!"

The hunchback took them to a window … and suddenly leapt out!

The children gasped and ran to the windowsill, expecting to see him fall. But no, there was a little ledge just below the window. Only Quasimodo could have known it was there!

"Phew," said Clara. "I was very worried!"

"See, he's not so scary," replied Beatrix, smiling. "Although, he seems a little unhappy, doesn't he? I bet he's lonely, up here in this tower all by himself."

"Don't forget his mates the gargoyles," joked Ben, pointing to one of the scary stone statues on the walls. "They're almost as ugly as he is!"

"Don't be cruel!" snapped Clara, and Ben lowered his head, ashamed.

Outside, the Hunchback was peering across the horizon from his ledge, one hand shielding his eyes from the sun. He had amazing balance, keeping only his toes on the ledge as he leaned over a two hundred foot drop holding onto just a single small gargoyle. The little bat-winged statue supported this acrobatic stranger, who spotted the hotel in just a few seconds.

"There – I knew I'd seen that name before! You can see the sign on the top of the building from here. Just follow the Quai du Marché Neuf up to the Sainte-Chapelle and bear right at the Pont Sainte-Michel."

Ben leaned in to Clara and whispered, "What does that mean?"

She replied, "Follow the riverside road up to the little church and turn right at the bridge. It should be easy to find it from here – but how are we supposed to sneak out of the cathedral without the teachers knowing?"

Quasimodo climbed back up from the ledge and crouched on the stone windowsill. The sunlight shone over his shoulders and through his thick hair, but even though the light was behind him they could still see his bright smile.

"I have an idea!" he said.

PART SIX: THE MYSTERIOUS MAN IN BLACK

"This is a crazy plan!" shouted Chris from the top of the Notre Dame's south tower.

The wind that had blown all across the city was now rippling their hair and clothes. They were two hundred feet high with the whole of Paris spread out below them like a map. They could see the roads of the island, and the blue waters of the Seine river branching and rejoining around it. It was very cold and windy at the top of the tower, so Chris wobbled a bit and had to hold onto Ben to stop from falling over.

Quasimodo said, "I can assure you, I have perfect balance. I've spent all my life exploring Notre Dame; I can run and jump over every part of it like a monkey! You'll be totally safe."

"If we want to do this, we have to trust him," said Clara, being brave at last. "Quasimodo, I trust you!"

"Good! Then please climb onto my back and hold on tight."

Clara did as she was asked. Then the strong Quasimodo asked for the other children to hold on too. Soon all four children were hanging onto the hunchback's strong shoulders and arms.

"Ready?" he called excitedly. "Here … we … *GO!*"

And he leaped off the top of the tower!

Quasimodo was indeed acrobatic. His strong feet caught every little ledge and crack in the side of the tower as he climbed down it. He moved far faster than a monkey in the trees of a rainforest. His strong hands gripped the bricks and ledges, and he had no trouble moving deftly with the four young detectives holding on to him. They all screamed as he jumped, spun and somersaulted down the side of the cathedral, running over its long arching buttresses, and leaping from windowsill to windowsill until he was almost to the ground.

Just when the children thought they could relax, Quasimodo leaped to swing from a lamppost, jumped to catch the branches of a tree, then ran through the tops of the trees with leaves and twigs brushing their faces.

The other visitors to the cathedral barely saw him; he was a whizzing blur, moving almost too fast to see. Some visitors reported seeing a giant ape at the cathedral, but others knew better: they were excited to tell people that they had seen the real life hunchback who had been in so many stories!

Meanwhile, the children hung on for dear life as their strong new friend soared from the trees onto the top of another building, then scampered over the chipped and broken rooftiles. He kicked away from a broken gutter, arcing over the street below like a bird, then landed on another building, where he put his four friends down at last.

They were breathless!

"That was better than a rollercoaster!" said Chris, throwing his arms up in the air.

"Thank you!" said Quasimodo gratefully. "I've spent so long cooped up in secret, that it's so great to have made some new friends. I can't thank you enough for being so kind, and not being frightened of my ugly face."

"I think you're very handsome!" said Beatrix, hugging Quasimodo. "You are so gentle and brave, it shines out of you! That's better than just being beautiful on the outside. Thank you for helping us."

"You're now on the roof of L'Hotel Notre Dame," said the hunchback. "I hope you find another clue to track down the thief. The Venus de Milo is one of the priceless treasures of Paris. Please find it again!"

"You aren't going to stay and help?" asked Chris.

"I'm sorry, I can't. I have to get back to Notre Dame to ring the bells at every hour. It's my one job, and I do love it dearly. I can't be late for any reason! But I wish you the best of luck, my friends! Goodbye!"

And with that, he jumped from the roof and scampered over the top of the neighbouring building, soon disappearing over the rooftops.

They were on the roof of the hotel. To get inside, they had to enter a door that led to a flight of stairs going down. On the way, they discussed how they might track down the man in black.

"We can't just go knocking on every door in the hotel," Clara pointed out. "What are we going to do?"

"We should ask at the front desk," said Ben. "I have a plan!"

They went all the way down the stairs and came out in the lobby, which had the shiniest floors that Ben had ever seen, and lots of pillars holding up the ceiling. There were huge potted plants with bright flowers, and some expensive-looking furniture designed for guests of the hotel to relax in.

The front desk was so big than Ben had to stand on tip-toe just to see over it. There was a stern-looking woman in a spotless uniform there to greet him.

"Um, bon-zhoor," he said, saying the French for 'hello': *bonjour*.

The woman seemed to sense that he spoke English, and so did him a favour. "Hello, young sir. How may I help you?"

"I'm looking for my Dad," said Ben, fibbing.

"Okay. What is his name?"

"Um, I don't know ... but he wears a long black coat and a black hat."

The woman looked at him suspiciously. "What's *your* name? You must have the same last names, yes?"

Ben realised that this plan wasn't going to work. He should have thought about it harder!

He apologised to the woman at the desk, then went around the corner to talk to his friends. "No go. She didn't buy it!"

"I'm not surprised," joked Chris. "She was probably offended at your terrible French speaking!"

"What are we going to do?" asked Beatrix.

Then they heard a familiar voice. It was a man's voice, speaking French very quickly: "*Bonjour mademoiselle, j'mappelle Commissaire Flambergé. Je recherche un suspect...*"

"It's that Detective!" said Beatrix. "I know – let's hide and see if he gets anywhere. Then we can follow!"

"Good plan!" said Chris.

They hid inside an open lift, with Chris stopping the doors from closing with his foot. They could hear the French Detective chatting with the woman, who seemed much friendlier with him than she had been with Ben. She opened a big box on the wall that was filled with keys, took one, and then left the desk. The Detective and two policemen followed her.

"They must know which room the thief's staying at!" said Clara. "They're coming this way! Hide!"

They ducked inside the lift. Luckily there were two lifts, and the Detective got into the other one.

"How do we know which floor they're going to?" asked Chris.

Clara smiled. "That's easy – watch the numbers on the little screen above the lift door!"

She was right: there was a small screen that showed a number. It went from 0 to 1 to 2… Finally it stopped on 5.

"They're on the fifth floor!" said Clara. "Quick, let's go!"

They pressed the number 5 in their lift, and the doors closed. The lift took them up, playing some gentle music. Beatrix recognised the song: it was called *Beyond the Sea*. It played at the end of one of her favourite films, one about a fish who gets lost in the ocean. She sang along, happy to know some of the words in French. She was starting to really like Paris!

When the lift gave a *ding!* and let them out, they were on the fourth floor, in a narrow corridor lined with lots of doors. They could see the woman from the desk, Detective Flambergé, and the two other policeman walking along the carpet. They stopped outside a door and began to knock and shout in French.

Suddenly there was a loud *BANG!* The door burst open, and the man in black jumped out at high speed! He shoved the Detective out of the way and ran down the corridor as fast as he could. He knew that the police had found him and wanted to get away. The policemen chased him, but at the end of the corridor he did an astonishing thing – he smashed a window and jumped outside!

"He'll fall and be as flat as a pancake!" gasped Clara. "That's not a very good escape plan!"

But to their astonishment, the Detective was shouting for the policemen to follow. There must have been a lower roof or staircase outside the window, allowing the thief to escape without falling. All three law enforcers climbed out the window after him, and disappeared from view.

This just left the startled desk woman. She looked into the room, shook her head, then hurried back towards the lifts. She got into the second lift and the doors closed.

"Phew!" said Ben. "They're all gone. But we were right about the man in black. He was definitely staying here."

"Let's look in his room," suggested Beatrix. "There might be more clues – or even the statue itself!"

They decided that they had no choice but to investigate!

They went inside the hotel room. It was a very expensive hotel, and so the room was quite luxurious. They guessed that the man must be expecting to make a lot of money when he sold the Venus de Milo. It was worth more than a King had in his treasure room.

There was the main room with a bed, desk and wardrobe, and another room which was a bathroom.

Ben went to look into the bathroom. He found a razor by the sink with some small hairs on it. There was also an empty container shaped like a number 8. Apart from these things, there was nothing else of interest.

In the main room Beatrix was looking around the bed. The sheets were crumpled and the pillows were in disarray. There was a small black book on the cabinet next to the lamp.

Chris and Clara examined the rest of the room. There was nothing that might be called a clue, except for a newspaper that had been folded up on top of the desk. There was a crossword puzzle with all the answers filled in. All the clues were written in French.

"Well, I think we have all the clues," said Chris. "Let's examine the evidence. What does it all mean?"

"The bed is very messy, as if he was tossing and turning all night," said Beatrix. "I don't think he could get to sleep. Maybe his guilty conscience is weighing down on him?"

"Maybe," said Ben. "And look, I found this in the bathroom."

It was the small container shaped like a number 8. It opened on a hinge and the inside was wet.

"That's a box for some contact lenses," said Clara. "You put them in your eyes so that you can see without needing glasses. My Mum wears them, but I don't like the idea of sticking something in my eyes! I'll stick with glasses, thank you very much."

Beatrix said, "I also found this notebook. It's a diary. On yesterday's date it says 'Eiffel Tower'. The day before just has a big X next to it. I think that shows the day he planned the burglary."

"What does today's date say?" asked Chris.

They looked at the little pages. "It says 'Sacré-Coeur, 5 o'clock.' What does Sacré-Coeur mean?"

"It's a place not too far from here," said Clara, who had been reading her tour information. She checked her phone for the time. "It's half past four! If we want to find out what his appointment was about, we'd better hurry!"

"We should leave the things where we left them, for the Detective," Beatrix pointed out. "It's not our place to take clues from a crime scene."

Just then, a stranger burst into the room. It was a tall, thin woman with an angry-looking face and short, choppy hair. "Who are you lot? What are you doing in our room?" she cried in surprise, her eyes going wide.

"Run!" said Beatrix.

The four friends dashed for the door to escape the woman. She swooped at them with her long arms, trying to catch them. She missed Beatrix by a hair's breadth, and when she turned to catch Chris she was too slow as well. Clara ran out behind her, joining the others outside.

The only person left in the room was Ben.

"I've got you, you interfering little brat!" shouted the woman with spit flying from her mouth. "This is none of your business!"

But she didn't know Ben! He was captain of the school football team, and went running with his Dad and neighbours several times a week. He was the sportiest of all of them! With a single run and jump, he leapt over the woman's sweeping arms and landed behind her in the corridor.

"Let's get out of here!" he shouted to the others, and they ran as fast as they could down the stairs and out into the street.

PART SEVEN: METRO MAYHEM
Outside, they ran around the back of the hotel to hide, panting from the exercise. Once they were sure that the frightening woman hadn't followed them, they began to put together a plan of action.

Clara told them about Sacré-Coeur. It was a building in the Montmarte area of Paris, a particularly beautiful type of building known as a basilica. A basilica is a type of church, but very different from the Notre Dame cathedral. It was made of white stone and very grand, standing at the top of a high hill, with three domed tower standing tall against the sky.

"What's the quickest way to get there?" asked Ben, jogging on the spot. He was so excited that he couldn't stop moving. Clara had to grab his shoulders and hold him down, or else he might have run right into the river before he could stop himself!

Clara said, "The quickest way must be the Metro. It's a bit like the London Underground."

"You mean, a train?" asked Chris, who loved trains. "What are we waiting for? Let's go!"

There was a Metro station very close by. There was a station near to all of the great tourist attractions in Paris. This particular station was for people who wanted to see Notre Dame, and was the only station on the little island. The children had seen the red and yellow METRO signs everywhere they had visited so far. It didn't take long to find.

The underground train station was, of course, under the ground. They had to take stairs down under the street to get there. But once they were inside the busy station, which was very pretty with white tiles and bright lighting, they realised that they would need tickets in order to get through the barriers.

"There's a ticket machine," said Beatrix. Luckily there wasn't a queue. The station was unusually quiet that day, perhaps because most Parisians were still at work at this time.

But the machine was in French!

"I can't work it!" said Beatrix.

Chris proudly took over. "If there's anyone who can get himself a ticket, it's me! Look, there's a button to switch to English…"

Luckily they had some French pocket money to hand. In France, the currency was the Euro, which many other countries in Europe used. Between them, they had enough money to get a ticket each.

They looked at a giant map on the wall of all the different stations in Paris, and how they were linked.

"I can't understand it," said Ben. "It just looks like spaghetti to me!"

"This is us in the SAINT-MICHEL NOTRE DAME station," said Chris, pointing. And we have to take this route to the stop called ABBESSES. I think that's the closest. I can't wait!"

"Why does he get so excited about trains?" asked Ben, baffled.

They found the correct place to wait, and soon enough they heard the sound of the train rumbling down the tracks towards them. A light shone from deep inside the tunnel, and a breeze picked up that ruffled their hair.

There was hardly anyone else on the platform with them, and they hadn't had time to look around. But when Clara did look, she got the fright of her life.

Just a few feet away, suddenly arriving in his coat and hat, was the man in black!

The train's brakes squealed as the train stopped. As the doors opened, passengers poured out and those waiting stepped in.

The car was almost empty. The children stood and held onto the rails. They all gaped when they saw the man in black jump through the beeping doors just before they closed.

As the train began to move away, Clara looked through the window and saw Detective Flambergé and his two officers, panting heavily. They must have chased the man in black here and missed him by a second!

"It's him!" whispered Ben.

"What do we do?" asked Chris, worried. "We can't stop him, he's too big!"

Clara had an idea. Just as the train began to pick up speed, she rushed to the open window and threw out the little black notebook. It landed on the platform near to the Detective, who stared at it in surprise. Then the train disappeared into the darkness of the tunnel, taking them away...

"I hope the Detective figures it out," said Clara. "Now he has the same clue that we had, and will hopefully follow us to Sacré-Coeur..."

"What about the man?" whispered Beatrix.

"We'll have to try to trap him and hope the Detective catches up. Otherwise, there are no more clues! The Venus de Milo will be lost forever!"

"Shhh!" said Ben.

The man in black was staring at them!

Had he heard them talking?

He must have realised something, because his face flickered from neutral to shocked, then to angry. He spun around and rushed away from the children, along the length of the train. When the children followed, he started to run.

"Where does he think he's going?" said Chris as they chased him. "He's on a train, he can't go anywhere!"

"We'll see about that!" shouted the man in black.

The train was already stopping. The man in black shoved his way through the people near the doors, then leapt out into the Abbesses Metro station. The Cluefinders ran after him.

"We can't lose him!" shouted Beatrix. "Don't let him out of your sight!"

They chased him through the barriers. They chased him up the stairs and into the sunlight. They chased him down the busy Parisian streets.

Soon they found themselves at the bottom of a very large hill covered in grass and trees. At the very top they could see the glory of the Sacré-Coeur basilica, looking like a beautiful white castle from a faraway land.

"We're here!" panted Ben, breathless. "He's running up the hill!"

They heard police sirens. A police car was racing down the street. It was Detective Flambergé! He must have understood Clara's message to him, and knew that the man in black had an important appointment here at Sacré-Coeur.

But the roads were busy and filled with people, and the man in black was already running up a steep path beside the hill. The children watched him duck into a narrow alleyway. When they followed, they saw that it was a dead end.

"We've got him trapped!" said Chris, celebrating.

Not only that, but three other men were trapped too!

Detective Flambergé caught up with them a few seconds later. At the end of the alley were four men. They each wore a black coat, and they each wore a black hat!

"Which one is the thief?" said the Detective, scratching his moustache. "We don't have enough people here to arrest all of them!"

"We can figure it out," said Beatrix. "We just need to look at the evidence."

They looked at each of the four suspects in turn. They thought they had been very clever with their disguises! They thought that no-one would be able to tell who was the real mastermind.

The first man had glasses and bright eyes, and a bristly chin.

The second man had no glasses, tired eyes, and a smooth, shaven face.

The third man had no glasses, tired eyes, and a bristly chin.

The fourth man had glasses, bright eyes, and a smooth, shaven face.

The Cluefinders tried to think of all the clues they had found in the hotel room: a razor with hairs on it, a box for contact lenses, and a messy bed from a sleepless night.

"We've got it!" said the Cluefinders together. "We know which one is the thief!"

PART EIGHT: THE REAL MASTERMIND

Detective Flambergé blurted, "Then please, tell ME! Which one is the real mastermind, and how did you know!?"

The four amateur detectives pointed confidently. "It's the third man! Arrest him!"

The policeman jumped on the third man in black. The others ran away before anyone could stop them.

"It doesn't matter about them," said Ben. "We have the right man here, I'm sure of it!"

The Detective looked inside the man's coat. Inside was an envelope filled with photographs of the Venus de Milo.

"So, you were here to try to sell the statue, were you?"

"How did you know it was me!?" screamed the thief. "It's impossible!"

"Not impossible," explained Beatrix. "It was simple. We saw your razor, which means the men with bristly chins couldn't have been the thief. We saw your contact lenses, so the men with glasses couldn't have been the thief either. Why would you wear glasses AND contact lenses? And we saw that you had tired eyes, because you'd been awake all night, which we knew from your messy bed."

The policemen put the man in black into handcuffs and put him in the police car. They had arrested him and were going to take him to jail for his crimes.

Detective Flambergé said, "Well done, you four! You would make excellent detectives when you grow up. I think the Mayor will make you friends of Paris for life after this!"

Then Clara replied, "I'm afraid it's not over yet, sir. There's one last person you need to talk to."

Even the other Cluefinders were surprised! "What do you mean, Clara?"

"We've forgotten one other clue that doesn't make sense," she said. "The crossword puzzle."

An hour later, Beatrix, Ben, Clara and Chris were back at the Louvre Museum. The Detective had driven them there, and he'd also called the teachers to tell them where the children were. Mister Faraday and Miss Marshall were very relieved. They came to the Louvre too to meet them.

They all stood in the long room where the Venus de Milo statue used to be. There were the four Cluefinders, the two teachers, Detective Flambergé, and the curator of the museum, Mister Gervais.

"It was very bad of you to run off like that," said Mister Faraday. "Your parents would never have forgiven us if you'd been hurt."

"But," said Miss Marshall, "we are very impressed about how you solved this crime."

"Absolutely!" said Mister Gervais. "I don't know what I would do if you hadn't captured the thief."

"But the Detective said that there was a final mystery?" said Miss Marshall.

"There is," Clara replied. "The mystery of the crossword puzzle. We all know that the man in black is English. And the Detective confirmed that the man doesn't speak a word of French, isn't that right, Detective?"

Detective Flambergé nodded. "That's correct, miss."

"If that's true, then how did the man complete a whole crossword, in French? We saw it in the hotel room. It's impossible! Unless ... he knows a very clever person, who happens to speak French. Someone who would also help him to steal the statue from this very secure museum. And I think I know who that friend might be."

"Who?" asked the Detective.

Clara pointed. "It's Mister Gervais, the curator!"

Mister Gervais went bright red. "B-but that's ridiculous! I'm not a criminal mastermind!"

"No," said Ben, realizing something, "but you *DO* love the Venus de Milo! A lot! I remember you telling us yesterday morning how wonderful it was. I think that *YOU* helped the man in black to steal it – for yourself! Everything else was just a performance!"

Clara nodded, smiling. "Detective, I think that if you went to Mister Gervais' house, you will find clues about where the statue is. You might even find the statue itself!"

"That is a total lie!" said Mister Gervais. "I love my job here! And even if my Venus really *IS* perfect and beautiful and angelic and wonderful, I couldn't possibly steal it!"

The Detective took out his handcuffs and looked seriously at Mister Gervais. "Well, I suppose we will just have to go to your house and find out, won't we?"

That evening, the whole class was in a fancy restaurant at the bottom of the hill. The sun had gone down, and they could see the Sacré-Coeur lit up against the night's sky like a glowing ice cream cone.

Mister Faraday and Miss Marshall made all the laughing, joking kids quieten down.

"Everyone, we have an announcement to make! Tomorrow morning we leave Paris, but tonight we have a special treat for everyone. We just got a phone call from the Parisian police force, who have confirmed that they have arrested both the thief and the mastermind who stole the Venus de Milo. Now the statue is back in the museum where it belongs. It's all down to four of our brightest students, Christopher, Beatrix, Benjamin and Clara, who used their brains and bravery to discover the truth behind the mystery. As a reward, everyone will be able to stay up late at the lodgings tonight and have extra dessert and hot chocolate!"

All the children cheered with joy, but none cheered louder than the Cluefinders!

—THE END—

ABOUT AUTHOR

Ken T Seth.

I love to write a customized story or a book for children.

I write inspiration, bed time story for make children smile.

My passion are anything about reading and writing.

Contact

Fanpage : https://www.facebook.com/kimaginepub

Website : www.k-imagine-pub.com

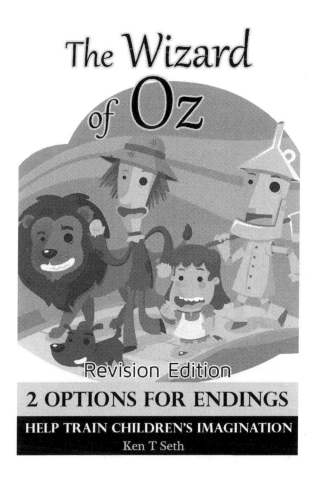

The Wizard of Oz

Revision Edition

2 OPTIONS FOR ENDINGS

HELP TRAIN CHILDREN'S IMAGINATION

Ken T Seth

Available at :
www.amazon.com/dp/ B00QJGFFAE

Hansel & Gretel

Revision Edition

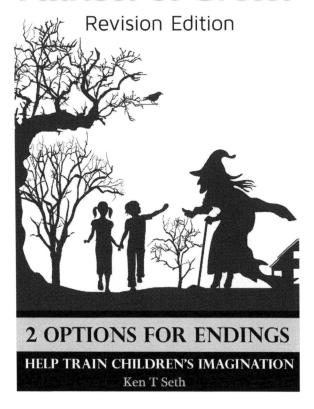

2 OPTIONS FOR ENDINGS

HELP TRAIN CHILDREN'S IMAGINATION

Ken T Seth

Available at :
www.amazon.com/dp/ B00SRU4G9G

Available at :
www.amazon.com/dp/ B00RGYE8NS

Made in United States
Orlando, FL
10 December 2022

25915691R00033